Skippy's Visit

Written and Illustrated by

Megan McCusker Hill

To my Bibble, my Beans, and my Boop -
Love you-
M.H.

ISBN: 978-1-7365907-1-3

LCCN 2021903196

Text copyright © 2021 by Megan Hill.
Illustration copyright © 2021 by Megan Hill. All rights reserved.
Published by Bibble and Beans Books, LLC., Mystic, CT.

Printed in the U.S.A.

This book is dedicated to my Grandma Skippy, a sweet delicate mixture of euphonious optimism and deep
appreciation,
with effervescent energy, and incalculable wisdom, who taught me that every moment is a gift. It is also for my boys, who daily keep me present, joy-filled, and open to the world.

Today I
ran
so fast...

past the willow
tree. I think she
waved at me.

I felt so happy
that I smiled back.

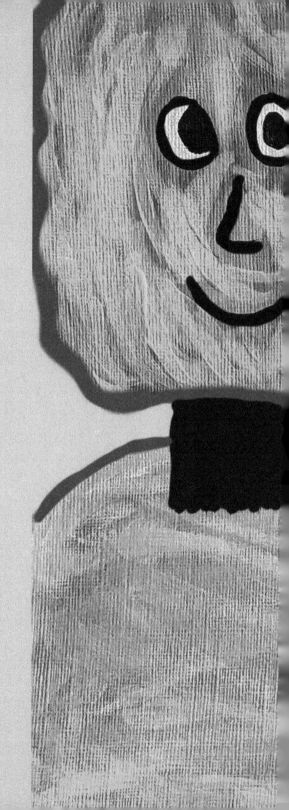

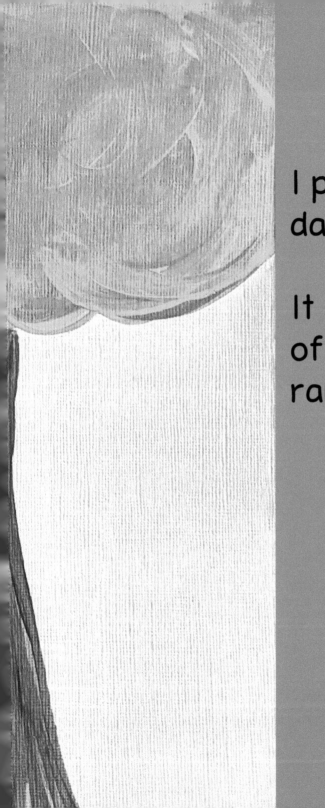

I played in the warm, dancing sunshine.

It seemed to bounce off of everything as I ran around.

Far back towards
the house, I could

hear my Dad calling for me. "Sprite, spriiiiiite...."

He looked very worried, "Sprite, Grandma is sick." I felt sad and scared.

Suddenly I couldn't feel the sunshine. A big cloud rolled in.

I flew to Florida so I
could see her,
and say goodbye.

That cloud followed me
all the way there.
My heart hurt in my
body and my tears were
bigger than raindrops.

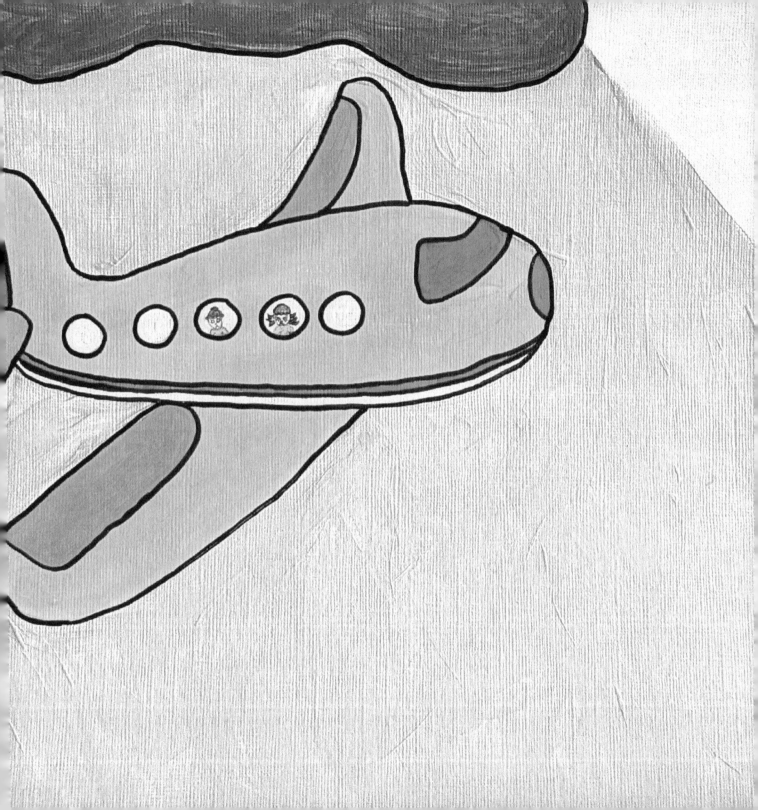

"Sprite," said Dad. "Grandma went to heaven."
"What is heaven?"
"It's a place where peace lives. It's where beauty lives."
"Then that is where Grandma should be," I said.

But, I was sad because I couldn't see her smile anymore.

The day after I learned Grandma went to heaven, my sister and I went to sink our toes in the sand and sit by the water. Grandma's memory swam in our minds as the sun warmed us.

We missed her and felt sad.
But, that day I learned something, as I sat
on that beach....

Sitting on the beach, and feeling so sad....
Out of nowhere, a dragonfly came and sat with
us, on my sundress. She sat there for a very
long time.

And even though she was so quiet, I knew this
dragonfly was my grandma. I could feel her.

As she sat there with us, I could feel a sense of peace and happiness wash over me.

That day I learned that beings in heaven could come down from above and visit us.

Heavenly beings could be with us again in a different form and sit with us.

If you ever feel sad about missing
someone who went to heaven,
look around at who,
or what,
is visiting you often.

Do you suddenly see ladybugs, or
red cardinals? Maybe you see bull-
frogs, or dragonflies, like me.

Your loved one might be here with you too.

Sometimes it is just a matter of looking.

This is the memorial bench created by my family to commemorate our Grandma Skippy. The beautiful artwork for the bench was done by my sister, Kelly McCusker, who was with me on the beach that day our Grandma visited us as a dragonfly.

The photograph of the beautiful dragonfly on the adjacent page is an actual picture of my Grandma Skippy that day after she passed away, on the beach, perched on my sundress.

Grandma Skippy
We sit at your bedside
Desperate to burn, every line of your face in our minds
every word, memory, moment we spent
near you
To inscroll these forever, within us
As the sheet rolls up and down with your labored breath
Our fear brings tears to our eyes,
pain of missing you, anguish in the void
unbounded cavernous suffocating hurt
we watch you teeter between worlds, aching for our loss
yet for a moment I remember, this travail belongs to me
you will fly now, unbroken, unfettered, interminable

and as you fly, I will sleep beneath the blanket you made me as a child
its mixture of flowers and safari animals much like who you are
a sweet delicate mixture of euphonious optimism and deep appreciation
a love of life in union with yawning devotion, effervescent energy, and incalculable wisdom

5-15-10 Megan McCusker Hill

Order 10+ books and receive a discount!

Contact Megan at Meganmccuskerhill.com for more information regarding your order.

MeganMcCuskerHill

MeganMcCuskerHill.com

ABOUT THE AUTHOR

Megan McCusker Hill is a scientist, professor, researcher, and author. Her career as a children's author was dreamed of as a small child and started to be brought to life after the passing of her Grandmother in 2010.

To learn more about the author and their work visit
meganmccuskerhill.com

CPSIA information can be obtained
at www.ICGtesting.com
Printed in the USA
LVHW070024300421
686057LV00013B/477